Katie Woo's
✳ Neighborhood ✳

SEP 2019

Stocking Up for the Storm

by Fran Manushkin

illustrated by Laura Zarrin

PICTURE WINDOW BOOKS
a capstone imprint

Katie Woo's Neighborhood is published by Picture Window Books,
A Capstone Imprint
1710 Roe Crest Drive
North Mankato, Minnesota 56003
www.capstonepub.com

Library of Congress Cataloging-in-Publication Data
Names: Manushkin, Fran, author. | Zarrin, Laura, illustrator.
Title: Stocking up for the storm / by Fran Manushkin ; illustrated by
    Laura Zarrin.
Description: North Mankato, Minnesota : Picture Window Books, [2019] |
    Series: Katie Woo's neighborhood | Summary: A big storm is
    approaching, and Katie, her parents, and all her neighbors head to
    the grocery store to stock up on necessities. At the store, Katie gets a
    lesson in smart shopping.
Identifiers: LCCN 2018059975| ISBN 9781515844556 (hardcover) |
    ISBN 9781515845553 (pbk.) | ISBN 9781515844594 (ebook pdf)
Subjects: LCSH: Woo, Katie (Fictitious character)—Juvenile fiction. |
    Chinese American families—Juvenile fiction. | Severe storms—Juvenile
    fiction. | Grocery shopping—Juvenile fiction. | CYAC: Neighborhoods—
    Fiction. | Storms—Fiction. | Family life—Fiction. | Grocery shopping—
    Fiction. | Chinese Americans—Fiction.
Classification: LCC PZ7.M3195 Sto 2019 | DDC 813.54 [E] —dc23
LC record available at https://lccn.loc.gov/2018059975

Graphic Designer: Bobbie Nuytten

Printed and bound in the USA.
PA71

Table of Contents

Katie's Neighborhood

Police

Library

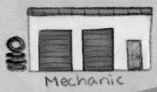

Mechanic

City Hall

Grocery Store

Post Office

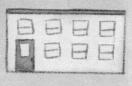

Chapter 1
A Big Storm

Katie was watching TV.

"A storm is coming," said the weather lady. "A big one!"

"Wowzee!" yelled Katie.

"The storm may last for days," said Katie's dad. "We need lots of food."

Katie agreed. "Lots of cookies!"

Katie's mom made a list.

"We need milk and cheese

and meat and fruit."

"And cookies," reminded

Katie.

The grocery store was crowded. Katie said hi to JoJo and Pedro.

"Don't worry," Mr. Nelson told Katie. "I've stocked up on everything."

Katie found the milk in the dairy section. She found chicken in the meat section.

"Good work, Katie!" said her dad.

Katie told her mom, "We need tomato soup too. If the storm is scary, tomato soup will cheer me up."

"Cookies and ice cream

cheer me up too," said Katie.

"Let's get both. Dad has a

credit card, so we don't have

to pay."

"I do have to pay," said Katie's dad. "I must pay when I get the credit card bill."

"Oh," said Katie.

"These cookies are on sale," said Katie. "Can we get them?"

"Yes," said her mom. "Smart shopper!"

Chapter 2

Getting the Groceries

Haley O'Hara and her five

brothers and sisters ran into

the store. They bumped into

a tower of toilet paper.

CRASH!

"Wow!" shouted Haley. "I'm glad it wasn't grape juice. Let's pile it up again."

"Cool!" said Katie. "It's like making a snowman."

Miss Winkle came in.

She told Katie, "I need food for my new puppy. His name is Twinkle."

Katie smiled. "He rhymes with you."

"Twinkle hates storms,"
said Miss Winkle. "He hides
under the bed."

"Oh," said Katie. "I hope
I don't need to hide under
the bed!"

Katie joined JoJo and Pedro at the checkout line.

"We got a lot of hot chocolate," said Pedro.

"I got spaghetti," said JoJo. "It's fun to eat!"

Chapter 3
Cozy at Home

Back home, Katie watched the wild wind shaking the trees.

She said, "I hope the birds' nests don't fall down."

Katie decided, "I need
tomato soup and grilled
cheese for dinner. And a
cookie for dessert."

It all tasted great!

"I hope my friends are okay," said Katie. She called JoJo.

"I'm painting. You should see the storm I made," said JoJo. "It's fierce!"

Pedro was loving his hot chocolate.

Haley and her wild brothers and sisters were making an angel food cake.

The storm went on for a long time. But everyone in Katie's neighborhood was safe and cozy.

Katie fell asleep with a smile. She dreamed that Mr. Nelson and his family were cozy too.

And it was true!

Glossary

chocolate (CHOK-uh-lit)—a food, especially a candy, made from beans that grow on the tropical cacao tree

credit card (KRED-it KARD)—a small, plastic card used in stores and restaurants to pay for items. Later, a bill is sent by the credit card company for all purchases made that month.

dairy (DAIR-ee)—if something is a dairy product, it is made with milk

fierce (FIHRSS)—bold and confident

neighborhood (NAY-bur-hud)—a smaller area within a city or town where people live and work

rhyme (RIME)—if words rhyme, they end with similar sounds

spaghetti (spuh-GET-ee)—long, thin strands of pasta made of flour and water and cooked by boiling

Katie's Questions

1. Explain why Katie's family and others went to the grocery store to stock up on food and supplies. Has your family ever done this?

2. Why do you think grocery stores organize items in sections, like dairy or meat? What would happen if items weren't organized?

3. Imagine a big storm was headed your way. Make a list of things you would need.

4. Mr. Nelson runs Katie's neighborhood grocery store, and he works with lots of people to make sure things run smoothly. Make a list of all the different types of jobs at a grocery store.

5. Would you like to work at a grocery store? Why or why not?

Katie Interviews Mr. Nelson

Katie: Hi, Mr. Nelson! Thanks for letting me come ask you questions about the store and your job!

Mr. Nelson: You're welcome! I love my job, and I love talking about the store.

Katie: Why do you love your job?

Mr. Nelson: Lots of reasons! I like leading the other store workers and helping them with their jobs. I like figuring out how much food and supplies I should order. I love getting to know all the people in our neighborhood. Sometimes I can help a customer find a certain ingredient or pick a perfect watermelon. I love that!

Katie: I love helping people too! Can you tell me more about ordering products?

Mr. Nelson: I order from food companies that deliver things by the truckload. I work really hard to get the amount right. If I order too little and run out of something, the customers will buy it somewhere else. Then the store misses out on making money. If I buy too much, it might get rotten before I can sell it!

Katie: Yuck! Sometimes I see teenagers working at the store. How old do you have to be to work in a grocery store?

Mr. Nelson: The rules are different depending on the store or what state you live in. At our store, you have to be 16. Stocking shelves or being a cashier is a great after-school job!

Katie: Just one more question . . . did you go to grocery-store college?

Mr. Nelson: Ha! Nope, I studied management at college. My classes taught me how to be a good leader and make good decisions for the store. But my friend who runs a store on the other side of town didn't go to college. He started working at a grocery store in high school. He did such a good job that his store kept giving him more responsibility. And now he runs the whole thing!

Katie: That's great! Thanks again, Mr. Nelson!

Mr. Nelson: You're welcome, Katie!

About the Author

Fran Manushkin is the author of Katie Woo, the highly acclaimed, fan-favorite early reader series, as well as the popular Pedro series. Her other books include *Happy in Our Skin, Baby, Come Out!* and the best-selling board books *Big Girl Panties* and *Big Boy Underpants*. There is a real Katie Woo: Fran's great-niece, who doesn't get into trouble like the Katie in the books. Fran lives in New York City, three blocks from Central Park, where she can often be found bird-watching and daydreaming. She writes at her dining room table, without the help of her two naughty cats, Chaim and Goldy.

About the Illustrator

Laura Zarrin spent her early childhood in the St. Louis, Missouri, area. There she explored creeks, woods, and attic closets, climbed trees, and dug for artifacts in the backyard, all in preparation for her future career as an archeologist. She never became one, however, because she realized she's much happier drawing in the comfort of her own home while watching TV. When she was twelve, her family moved to the Silicon Valley in California, where she still resides with her very logical husband and teen sons, and their illogical dog, Cody.